CW00435637

The Widov

Collection of Stories
Book I

By: Scott Jenkins

Copyright © 2018 by Scott Jenkins

Scott Jenkins Publications

All rights reserved. This book or any portion thereof may not be reproduced or used in any manner whatsoever without the express written permission of the publisher except for the use of brief quotations in a book review. The characters in this book are purely fictitious. Any likeness to persons living or dead is purely coincidental.

Food for thought:

"Satanism is about worshiping yourself, because you are responsible for your own good and evil"
(Marilyn Manson, The Long Road Out of Hell)

"The effect of religion has been to cherish this conceit by making men think that the universe invariably conspires to support the good and bring the evil to naught. By a subtle logic, the effect has been to render morals unreal and transcendental."
(John Dewey, Human Nature and Conduct)

"This...is God."
(Freddy Krueger, A Nightmare on Elm Street)

"Live or die. Make your choice."
(Jigsaw, Saw)

Introduction: The Widow Forest

The Widow Forest is a place consumed by fear and evil. A Cellar Door rests deep within Widow Forest, far from wandering ears, and eyes. An entity able to devour twisted souls in the most wicked of ways waits for victims listens for footsteps and rapid heartbeats, happening upon the Cellar Door. Reaching the door requires travel through darkness under a thick canopy of trees and crowded brush, a venture that brings prey face-to-face with predator. When silence is broken, filled by the shrill shriek of the door slowly swinging open a nightmare escapes – the prey's nightmare – hungry for torture and death. Only those with clear, innocent intentions are saved from a hellish fate, or even baring witness to the door's inhabitant.

The dark aura surrounding Widow Forest is undeniable, regardless of physical proof. The legend alone keeps most from traveling toward, even the edge of the forest, for fear of being absorbed by the darkness which resides. However, some choose to tempt fate and dance with everlasting judgment: those that throw caution to the wind, those too filthy to fear what waits within. Dishonorable, damaged souls boldly ignoring the power of this ominous forest, this legend, and a sign warning all to...

Stay out! The Widow Forest awaits its next victim!

Stacey

Stacey was a good girl. Fully-grown at sixteen-years-old standing a mere five-foot-one, she was cursed to be forever considered *little one* by her family. Didn't matter she was the eldest child. Her life was spent being Mommy and Daddy's precious, little angle. Nothing could sway her dedication to living life *by the book*. More than anything else, she loved being her parents *little one,* their dependable one.

She refused trial against her morals. Even Tiffany, Stacey's longest and best(est) friend, was discarded for actions against the *good girl* book. They shared a common obsession with Hello Kitty, Chad Michael Murray, and other girly things for so long. But a ten-year friendship came to an end as abruptly as sleep to a demanding alarm clock when Tiffany started using foul language.

Stacey wondered when Tiffany switched from liking Chad's smile to wondering how large his cock was. But she was one, Tree Hill Raven to proclaim *never more!* Tiffany pierced Stacey's soul with immature glares as their mothers discussed the gross language and slutty notions Tiffany poured to Stacey. Luckily, the snotty comments at school, and evil glares could not pierce Stacey's *suit of armor* made of *holier than thou* material.

She lived by the rules and *fuck* anyone who didn't – she could think it, just not say it.

All was not lost, she still had her brothers. If no one wanted to be her friend, she would simply ensure the younger heirs of her family maintained decent course through life. Whether it was homework, chores, or other tasks she always came to the rescue. Kevin even got an *A* on a science project she helped complete a few years back. Dad was busy with work and Mom was overcome with Book Club, so she answered the communal call—always dependable Stacey. She could hold her nose high, snubbing all those at school unable to attain her status. No one would detach her mind, body, or soul from being the ever-awesome *little one*.

She *was* a good girl.

All good things come to an end, even Stacey's *goodness*. Hormones get the best of any teenager, boy or girl. Unfortunately, Stacey's hormonal spike attacked after Tiffany's. Maybe if it hadn't Stacey would have understood, or even, been able to lean on another about her overwhelming desire for Chris. Stacey's thoughts were consumed with wonder about the sweetness of his lips.

She was shocked that the price for tasting Chris's lips was her innocence, by force. A serpent slithered between her legs as a beast held her to the ground. Her first kiss shared with a demon rather than a prince. A kiss she knew to be scandal took its payment without regard. Chris left her on the ground, broken and shattered. The echoes of his laughter haunted her evermore, reinforced each time she passed him at school. Her essence held hostage behind the fly of his trousers.

She did well-enough hiding the transformation that occurred to her being in each passing day. Smiling sweetly as she's retreated into her bedroom, allowing fear and turmoil to grow beneath the surface. She started taking dinner in her bedroom, instead of at the table as always expected. First, claiming schoolwork required her undivided attention and time, then hobbies in exchange. Before long she had adjusted the norm, and no one questioned. She traded four family members for, four-walls.

Hell, school was even easier. Realization hit like a punch to the gut: Had anyone ever paid attention to her? Teachers almost seemed happy for her new-found silence. She was invisible in building of over 300 people. No, she wasn't invisible. She was ignored – the whole world was full of demons. The fear, pain, and turmoil evolved into a wretched darkness – the only voice she could hear.

Was the world always a lie? Had she always been an annoyance that others wished to simply ignore? Had her family only loved her as a damned formality? A formality easily overlooked with simple excuses and fake grins. The darkness sank its teeth into her being with each passing realization unlike any emotion or person ever had. There was solitude in her new friendship with darkness that was equally comforting as painful. The kids at school didn't want her – fine. Her family continued without her – also fine. Chris didn't want her – fuck him. Obviously, the world didn't want her either, right? So, she clung to her darkness, the truest friend she ever had.

Before long Stacey was drained of all her goodness, food offered to the darkness, but it demanded more. The cries for *more* kept the Sandman from visiting Stacey; either that or even sleep was scared of this particular version of *darkness*.

One night, she could no longer ignore its call for play and drug a blade across her thigh. The blood tickled her skin as it ran down her leg. The pain faded, and she released a relaxing sigh. Blood met full travel on the floor and the darkness assured her its craving was met. Her reward: a restful night of sleep.

Stacey was a woman now, Chris made sure of that, so it was only fair she unwinds the way adults did – her drink of choice: vodka. It was definitely an acquired taste; but before long her face didn't even purse when she took a long swig. Darkness praised the choice. Drinking numbed the memories of better days, or any notions of doubt. She became *friends* with all the *right* people, those able to supply her with booze and test answers. Who cared about a couple lifted twenties from Mom's purse or a random handjob? She and her best friend were happy, nothing else mattered. Weeks of drink left her mentally and physically numb to the world. Perhaps that's why it's illegal to drink and drive.

She never meant to hit somebody.

Her nightly routine was interrupted when the vodka bottle clanked against the ground empty, announcing its retreat from the festivities. Sleep wouldn't come if she couldn't obtain proper buzz. Logic drifted away into the night sky, much like that of any normal person after drinking, but more so since *she* was drunk-off-her-ass. She *needed* another drink. The four walls spun, laughing at her predicament. How could she be so stupid, letting her supply empty? Maybe there was a spare bottle hidden in the closet – no luck. There was only one option: she snuck out of the residential sanctuary called *home* to drown the voices bellowing her unworthiness to live, to capture sleep for one more night.

There was a spot, where teenagers could buy alcohol without worry of entrapment. Perhaps she was invisible to the world close to her, but there was no reason to tempt fate with the likes of law enforcement. But she had to travel into the abyss of lowlife scum to get her fix. The stench assaulted her nose the moment she stepped out of her car. The smell accurately described the scene: Teenage boys that hadn't showered in weeks, half-smoked cigarettes, and women with half-exposed nips and a complete lack of self-worth. Good girls wouldn't be caught dead in such situations, yet her she was. She couldn't stand the types of people that surrounded her in this new life. But was she any better? Was she in any position to judge? Her fate was solidified, all because of Chris. At least he gave her the darkness as a parting gift. The darkness would make everything better. She simply needed a drink. Then she could disappear again.

She trekked through the cloud of toxic smoke and wretchedly loud music – something about bitches and hoes – toward her goal: Chelsea, a young adult who loved tainting youth. Stacey hated the bitch or at least the sight of her. Chelsea would let the teenage boys fondle her like a game controller, a sight that sickened Stacey. But maybe Stacey really hated her because one day she would be her. She paid for her vodka and trudged back to the car.

As the vodka ran down her throat, Stacey ignored all thoughts once more, only concerned with the warm, numb sensation it offered. The night sky was glittered with stars. Back roads made for the best night rides, the lack of lights allowed clear vision of the sparkly sky. When Stacey was younger her dad would take her on car rides in the middle of night – just the two of them. They would listen to old Rush tracks and stare at the sky. He would tell her about how much he loved the music and sharing it with her. She hated the singer's voice but loved the father-daughter time. How long had it been since they went on a car ride?

She maintained one hand on the wheel and turned the bottle up, downing the medicine, coating the reopened emotional wound. With each gulp the voices faded to background noise. Slowly her father's smile floated away, replaced with the warm suffocation of darkness – something she was more comfortable embracing. Her mind, body, and soul shared a common trait: disorientation – mission success. All she had to do was get back home, the same way she had driven time again, and she would be rewarded with sweet, silent slumber.

Her nerves began shutting down, one-by-one, starting from her finger tips, and then inward toward her body mass. The fog inhabiting her brain clouded realization of the disorientation. She was on a timer that was slowly switching off for the night, with each passing second, another sense compromised. Her mind flooded with calming waves. Her eyes fluttered her minds last attempt at hard reboot. Thoughts of sleep captivated the last of her wits, leaving no caution for the road – or anything, really. Her mind jump-started when the car thumped against obstacle on the road.

Her body revitalized, a second wind seemingly cleared sleep and alcohol from her wits. Nerves sparked to life, raising the hair across her body. The car was still traveling in correct alignment, so what happened? Mental debate cross-examined the situation. The car hit something, or maybe someone. The idea alone filled her eyes with tears. Stacey balanced the wheel with her knee, freeing her hands. The goosebumps on her skin *had* to go. She waved off the faint sounds of screaming like an annoying fly. The darkness wanted her to feel even worse about herself, but this was too much. Why would someone be walking in the road, in the middle of the night, no less?

Stacey had her own issues to deal with. Her mind returned to autopilot, only focused on the silent ride back home. Fuck the stars, fuck rush, and funk whatever was in the road.

The driveway appeared, and with it, everything else disappeared. Safety was a mere fifteen feet away, and with it, her bed. The darkness carried her drunken body in the house, up the stairs, and into her bed without alarming other occupants. She drifted into a drunken slumber; the last shred of her soul evacuating, leaving only darkness to fill the void. There was no shred of goodness left or hope for its return.

****

"Stacey! Wake UP!"

Stacey used her hands to wipe sleep from her eyes. She kept her hands there, keeping the pounding in her head at bay.

"Get out of my room, I'm sleeping!" She replied, one of her asshole brothers was invading a much-needed REM cycle.

"Get the fuck up!" Commanded Not-One-Of-Her-Brothers.

Her eyes fluttered open, light was attacking her brain. Adjusting to the light eased the pain but offered anew. Standing at the foot of her bed was her father. His demeanor was different than ever before. She had never seen him so angry, and tears running down his face added effect. The calm and loving person, she had always known, gone, probably forever – just like his *good girl.* He was fidgeting, sweating, and crying, adding to the uncomfortable stench in the air – or was it the liquor from her skin? Each fingertip had spots of red where he had pulled skin and nail off, but he continued. Even as she stared at him, he kept pulling chunks away with only slight grimace of pain.

"Look, Dad, sorry." Stacey started. "I thought you were one of the boys. What's wrong?" She asked. She didn't need an answer. It was obvious she had been drinking, one of the boys probably smelled it and tattled – little shits. All she could do now was hope the yelling would wait till later, when her hangover ended.

He looked around the room in silence; hiding whatever question he had behind his tear-filled eyes. Stacey grew angry, clenching at her sheets to stay calm. Who was he to judge her? Where had he been all this time?

"Stacey, I need to know what happened." He finally choked out. He zeroed in on her, the tension grew, and both gave way to uncomfortable electricity in the room, jittering left-and-right.

Stacey snapped. She wasn't going to be judge. Chris was the bad one. She simply was living out his punishment.

"Look, okay, like, I know I'm drunk, but you don't have a right to be in her so get the fuck out!" She screamed.

Her father stared, tears streaming down his face faster than he could wipe them away. A small part of Stacey wanted to hug him. To feel like his *little one* again, but it was too late for that.

"I know you're drunk," He stumbled. "I want to know why the car is covered in dents and blood!"

They attempted breath, in silence. Stacey tried to remember, her head constricted in response warning her to wait a bit for such activities. She could have sworn it was a dream, she wouldn't hit someone – couldn't hit someone. She protested the event, frantically shaking her head hoping to dislodge a missing piece of the puzzle, and with it, a clear conscious.

"No what, Stacey?" He prodded. "Tell me what happened! Tell me this is all a misunderstanding." He reached for her arm, offering a fatherly embrace – offering comfort and security.

She flinched, offering only a snarl.

"What happened to you, Little One?"

"Look, please, just get out, and let me think!" She cried out, not only to him, but also to the darkness residing inside. She took a breath, health class taught her intentional breaths calmed situations like this – it wasn't working. Dad wasn't budging, her convulsion and deprivation solidified his position—she needed help, she needed her daddy. But she didn't; what she *needed* was a damn minute. The clock caught her eye while dodging her father's – it couldn't truly be three in the afternoon. She defaulted to muscle memory in the interest of time.

"Dad, can I just have a minute alone to get dressed. I want to talk to you, but I just need to clean up, and get my head straight."

Dear-ol'-dad couldn't fight the shift in demeanor, for a moment his daughter returned, the sweet smile and loving eyes. He left the room with a faint smile, playing part in Stacey's plot. He turned from the door and confessed with the deepest sincerity, "I love you, Little One."

"I know Dad. I promise it will be okay." She responded and waved a hand for expedited privacy.

He turned back to the hall tears streaming unwittingly giving privacy, *not* to his daughter, but to the darkness controlling her. A mistake he would take to an early grave: the worst he ever made.

The door latched shut and Stacey sobered in mind, but her body hadn't received the memo. The bed sheets flew to the floor as she launched to the closet for a bag and essentials. There was no way Dad was going to let this go. She needed to disappear, it had been so long since anyone noticed her: she didn't like the attention. Bolting from corner-to-corner of her room, she gathered the pertinent items. Cigarettes-and-lighter, check. Two outfits, check. The remainder of alcohol, a box of razors, cell phone—no one said teenagers were smart – and her favorite book, *Jonathan Livingston Seagull...check*. All she ever wanted to do was play it safe, fly straight and steady. But now she was in a barrel roll, diving toward the Earths hard embrace and it wasn't going to be pretty. She and the darkness agreed, it was time to leave. It was time to become invisible again. Besides, whatever she hit the night before was a situation not worthy of her presence. Everything else was handled without her present – why couldn't this be the same? Bag packed, she opened her window. Vomit pooled in her mouth as the ground rippled to-and-fro below. She was no pro and her head was still woozy, but she had no choice.

She had to jump. Regardless of the distance or consequence, she needed to plummet to the ground just, like her life already had.

The ground broke her fall taking her breath as payment, her chest tightened, and she gasped frantically, without air to her lungs panic took control. She rolled over surveying the area for wandering. No one saw – or heard. She took a moment to catch her breath. She was about thirty seconds behind on air intake since the jump. Someone could have heard her landing – smooth as it was – so she reignited the fire to get the hell away.

She was not a good girl, she had done horrible things and if anyone saw her, she wouldn't be able to hide the horrendous actions seeping from her face. The disappointment, filth, and sin oozing from every pore. No amount of showering would hide it from the world. She slowly picked up speed, putting one foot in front of the other like *the little fuck-up that could.* Her eyes deviated from the course long enough to notice the family car in the driveway, specifically the horrific damage. What felt like a simple bump the night before was exposed under the harsh rays of daylight: The front bumper was no longer a smooth chrome mold. Instead it was dented, mangled even, and covered in blood. The driver side front tire was mostly deflated, the rim scrapped, dirty, with hair lodged between rim and rubber. The worst of all hit in-tow commanding notice, the smell. The smell of burnt hair and flesh. An unseen cloud of verified death. What organism could have survived such a collision? If she did kill someone, instead of something, life would be getting a lot harder – all because of Chris. So, she ran, away from home, away from the car, away from reality into the cold embrace of darkness.

Blame for the entire ordeal belonged solely on Chris's shoulders. She hated him for what he did and for how he changed her. Her essence, her innocences, her *goodness,* all taken by him and were no different than the putrid smell coming from the family car.

What began as an escape plan evolved into a revenge mission – Chris would have to pay for his actions, and hers. Chris killed her and as a result killed something, or someone else. He had to die before someone else faltered into his grasp. She had to find Chris and make him pay for all of this, then she would leave town, finally able to start a *new* life. She would live her final days drunk waiting for the darkness to devour her, but first Chris had to die.

Stacey stopped a few blocks away from home, in the large, open field on the outskirts of the Royal Grant housing development. The field had offered seclusion for Stacey many times before. Dead center of the development rested a flat, lush green field big enough for a person to easily hide from eyes on the road. The field was typically empty, no kids ran amok, which could be why no one really paid attention to it. Honestly, the only other person Stacey remembered ever being there was Scott. He would lie on the ground talking to himself – or his imaginary friend, as the rumors tell. Stacey always left him alone: they had an unspoken understanding and mutual respect for the field, plus she didn't want to *actually* talk to the freak.

She released a loud sigh, stress lifted from her shoulders as she reached the furthest edge of the field. Hell, Scott wasn't even there at the moment; she had heard about him starting some geeky pen-and-ink adventure with his friends—devil worshiping shit, she would swear it. Regardless, she knew the

18

field and its trees offered much needed shroud while she made her phone call. She needed to call Chelsea and ask a favor, or demand if necessary. With one last survey for privacy she hit call and waited for an answer.

"Hello?" Announced a groggy voice with crackling cell reception.

"Chelsea, what are you doing?" Stacey began, offering cordial small talk with a noticeable tone of, *wake the fuck up*.

"It's too early, I'm going back nigh-night." Chelsea responded.

If Stacey had never seen Chelsea – and proof of age by way of driver's license – then her telephone skills would make her think she was no older than a fucking toddler.

"I need to know where Chris is, can you text him and find out?" Stacey wasn't in the mood for her games—straight to the point.

"Okay, jeeze. I think he is taking his girly-friend to the dumb, spooky forest you guys talk about all the time. Must be hibbidy-dibbidy time."

If possible, Stacey would have choked Chelsea through the phone for the chuckle that coupled the comment. Instead she took a deep breath, remembering she was talking to a fucking idiot.

"So, they are going to Widow Forest? Fine, that works," Stacey recapped. The sounds of some young man suckling

Chelsea made Stacey's skin crawl. "Chelsea, you're a fucking pedo, get a life you piece of shit."

Chelsea attempted to respond, but Stacey had already hung up and dropped the phone to her side. She was sure Chelsea would get her's, sooner or later. But for now, Chris was her only concern—the predator becomes the prey.

Several hours passed, afternoon turned to evening, then to night, while Stacey stood at the edge of Widow Forest. The damned forest of so many childhood stories. In fact, she had never been this close to the forest for fear of some dark evil looming inside, thoughts rooted from the stories passed in the community. So, either the stories weren't true, or she – against better judgment—had aligned with the morally corrupt and ignorant. Countless times she questioned her mission but the darkness that consumed her soul kept her poised for execution. She could simply leave, take her hurt and drown sorrow elsewhere. Maybe even get over the pain within over time. But the pain and darkness consumed her, reminding her of his demented act. Of how he smirked at her around every corner. How a few times he even brushed against her, as if her body was his property, available for molestation at will.

No, she would wait, and he would pay. The night sky hid Stacey's presence but, little did she know, she wasn't hidden from the true predator. As she waited for Chris, something was waiting for anyone to stumble upon judgment.

Chris was close, the smell of his repugnant cologne penetrated Stacey's nostrils. He was with his girlfriend, Sarah: Sarah had no idea the evil she allowed to grope her massive tits and tight ass. Or maybe she did. Either way, the rage grew and Stacey needed to know why Sarah received the sweet kisses from Chris that she longed for in the past? Why was Sarah allowed to play the innocent game of cat-and-mouse without the terrifying end? No, Sarah wouldn't have her life changed – she wouldn't be giving blowjobs in the locker room for alcohol – she wouldn't be stealing money from any unsuspecting person for goods. No, Sarah would get to play pretty princess and be a *good girl* with Chris – well fuck her! But Stacey wasn't concerned with Sarah's well-being, all she cared about was revenge. She already killed something—or someone—and if Sarah got in the way, she would die, too.

Perhaps Sarah knew what Chris did with Stacey. Or more accurately what he did *to* Stacey – Stacey's blood boiled. The idea of jokes, or pleasure at her expense discoursed the plan – they both would die.

Stacey kept her position, shrouded behind trees and the dark night sky watching the couple slip behind a mossy curtain, past the old weathered sign, ignoring the urban legend of doom-filled terror. That sign would need an update after Stacey completed her task, perhaps she would update it herself with Chris's blood using his severed dick as the brush. She was going to give the town one more reason to believe in monsters and fairytales. Blood would paint the trees, removing all doubt of Widow Forest's power.

Stacey's wicked smile shifted the air. Woodland creatures scurried away as if naturally aware of an evil presence. However, not of Stacey's, but of the evil out for her.

Stacey waited an obligatory three(ish) minutes before following into natures domicile. Throwing caution to the wind, void of the fact that she was headed the proper into evil's grasp.

Over-abundant swigs of vodka contorted her sense of direction into that of a toddler. She bounced off trees like a drunken pinball: left-then-right, to-and-fro, all over the damned place. But, Stacey didn't mind the rough, scraping embrace of each tree – it was better than the wandering digits of devilish serpents like Chris.

Before long, the state of her travel prompted a *tilt*. She needed a break from both walking and drinking. The night sky shaded insecurities and faulty judgment. Surely in the light of day such actions and plots – like following a rapist into a dark forest and planning a double homicide – would meet swift debate, and termination. As if the light of day demanded realization, like a mirror. Instead the dark-of-night shroud. Offered a cold chill, freezing – slowly – her body, mind, and soul. Then, her body turned numb locking the insanity below an ice-cold shell.

Widow Forest housed many oversized trees covered in fluffy green moss, the type that felt *just* as nice as Dad's recliner, at least in this moment they did – Stacey needed no more than a single moment to rest.

She hit the ground – *thud.* And released a sigh. Being grounded was perfect for inspecting the path ahead and behind. How could she be expected to properly pursue her prey when the forest wouldn't stop spinning?

She had a scary realization. A lump in her throat. A racing heart. Every once of her being heard loud-and-clear what her mind discovered…

She was lost.

A punch to the throat left her gasping for breath – panic's way of saying *hello.* Her knees gave way, no matter, all energy was focused on inflating her lungs and stopping the world from spinning.

Nature stared from shadowed brush with judging eyes – fuck a pretentious bunny rabbit. A beetle crawled across her hand, "Fuck off me," Stacey screamed from her sweat soaked lips. Her head rocked from left-to-right, repeatedly testifying her discontent – the physical response would cease her heart from attempting escape.

New vantage was the answer, had to be, she dug hard into the ground and hoisted her drunk self up. Stacey stood as tall as possible, tippy-toes and all, peeking through darkness and thick brush, hoping for some form of comfortable familiarity beyond the fearful night. No such luck – of course a mere three-feet wouldn't help. A quick subconscious game of *eeny-meeny-miny-moe* determined a random path, plausible as any other for pursuit – blind faith for the win, Alex.

Fear stole away Stacey's wits, her ability to decide, properly, so she was left with nothing other than primitive decisions without thought. Never before had she felt so alone, yet so investigated by surrounding darkness.

The forest made sure to make its presence known by way of her heightened fear. The bugs latched to her skin, attempting theft of blood from vein. Ten bugs to be accurate. Trackable because her skin stung with raised welts where she assaulted herself with each attack. If she could just reach a lit area, a place of safety, but they appeared in the distance and disappeared just past her eye and travel her tears and wails echoed through the trees, returning against her as if laughter to her fear. Her skin hard, painfully tight, as the goosebumps grew atop her body, her bodies visual result of fear.

The forest was toying with her, pushing the alcohol out— replacing it with 100-proof fear. With heart and mind out-the-door, the only remaining thing was for her body to *get-the-memo and* join the evacuation.

To late.

Her body froze, unable to command limb. She put her head on a swivel—the only thing she could, physically do. Perhaps the air would carry a morsel of hope her direction- a sound, a voice, something, anything—a breadcrumb laced path leading her away from the abysmal darkness she unwillingly inhabited.

No such luck.

The harder she attempted to listen for Serenity's call, the louder her heart pounded, voiding any other sound from her ears.

"Hello!" She screamed. Only blind-luck and faith left to rely upon.

A faint voice in the distance called back: *help me.* She was sure it was a girl, close by—*maybe it was Sarah?* Regardless of prior engagements or plans, Stacey just needed another human being in her company. Her body needed the company, her mind needed the comfort of diminished solidarity.

"I'm coming, stay there!" She replied, chasing the distant voice. Even if the girl was also lost strength in numbers would prevail – right? And so Stacey ran, with a new found clarity. She would find the fleeting voice and the two would stay in touch for a lifetime, talking about the chance meeting they shared, lost in Widow Forest. Spend the wonder years telling grand-children about how they survived the urban legend, thusly, producing an

unwavering bond, making them the *best(est)* of best friends –
BFFs for life: shrub-in, shrub-out type shit.

Stacey wasn't going to stop for anything, her new
(best)friend was out there in need of help. Hell, even an oddly
large pig running in the distance didn't sway her course. Her
mind tried to derail as her body continued – a pig in the middle
of the forest? Her footing stuttered, her mouth agape, forehead
wrinkled. But, she forced brain and limb back to unison, and on
task. Piggy might not have been indigenous to the area, but...

Porky could fend for himself.

So, she ran, aimlessly toward her unknown companion.
Mind, body, and soul on board with the plan. This mystery
woman would bring freedom, friendship, and possibly –
hopefully – a return of *the good girl* Stacey once was. She could
be the hero of this story, no, she *would* be. She could be the one
that saves a life, as easily as she would have taken one mere
minutes before. If her *goodness* could be taken in under 5-
minutes, why couldn't it return in the same fashion? Just maybe,
everything wasn't lost.

She wasn't moving fast enough. The vices of her
transformation holding her back from full sprint. She released
her bag and took off, full sprint engaged, leaving behind the
secondary tools of her destruction. No matter, absolution was
ahead, fuck the life and choices she carried – all would be
forgiven. If it wouldn't't've been weird she would have stripped,

making herself supremely aerodynamic. But that would have been the making of a bad first impression.

The trees thickened, the path narrowed, the brush forcibly slowed Stacey's assault. Multiple branches and roots became obstacle requiring tactical evasion if she was to find her friend. Stacey never was one for PE class, once she was excused from such activities simply to avoid embarrassment. Her teacher was more than willing to oblige since most of the period would have been spent listening to why such activity was necessary for success in life. But barrel rolls, low crawls, and hurdle jumps seemed to come easy in this scenario, jocks made it seem so difficult, but it really wasn't. She was making the forest her bitch, at least that is how she saw it, she was poised to be the hero of Widow Forest. A new legend in the making

The path ended, almost as quick as began, and Stacey crossed the finish line like a drunken gymnast. Her limbs ached in the chilly air, a recent development with a free moment on the ground. Her travels didn't come without consequence. Her limbs covered in scrapes and cuts, but in her wake laid the trimmings of Widow Forest's bushes and trees: both sides housed casualties that day.

Room to breathe, a wonderful thing, and one that Stacey questioned as a perplexing turn. The trees had cleared into an open meadow, giving way to the open night sky, starlit and clear.

Between air and breeze her nerves gave rest. Beauty was housed in the middle of Widow Forest, a calm before the storm.

She rose to her feet examining the area for a wicked undertone, or perhaps her lost, future friend. Open space was nice, but how did she get in? Behind her, and on all sides, there didn't seem to be a clearing. No way out of this glorious meadow. No obvious entry or exit, as if she was born and raised inside the eerie, yet beautiful meadow.

The meadow floor, a vibrant emerald green, the grass and moss appearance enhanced by the moon above. Stacey was in awe of the sight but something deep inside was screaming, danger. Stacey wasn't going to be the next Dorothy, obviously she would be able to decipher danger, the night was simply confusing her senses.

However.

Making break from the foliage, formed to the ground as if natures creation rested the most particular of door – The Cellar Door, to be exact. The door was molded from weathered wood, but instead of appearing installed, or placed, roots dug deep into the ground and claimed solid foundation for the door. The door was a living piece of the forest. Splinter and swirl decorated the door with a terrifying beauty. If such a thing was produced from the Earth's core: what was birthed from within?

Funny how in life so many things happen, simultaneously, leaving question of sequence and causation. Kind of like when the ground rumbled, and Stacey fell to her knees, simultaneously. But that's impossible, no cause-and-effect, just cause-and-cause leaving her praying for the dream to end and for all the questions and calamity to follow suit. She bowed her head and asked a supreme being to save her from nightmarish things. What was *really* happening, none of this fit reality – a common thought in her recent history. Chris stole away her innocence, and with it the normal life she was accustomed, now she lived a life full of *this can't be real,* type shit.

Stacey raised her head from the ground, streaked with tears, and watched in fear as the Cellar Door splintered open. The eerie, beauty from moment s before cracking and decaying before her eyes. The planks twisted under pressure and shot about like hellish arrows from a demon's bow. Stacey took augmented cover: pushing her body into the earth to avoid impalement. Her skin numbed from the sound reverberating around, or maybe she was already dead, and feeling was gone forever. At least then, the nightmare would be over.

Just like with so many other things in life, she waited the obligatory three(ish) moments after silence returned, then looked up.

A single hand pulled from beneath the surface, crushing more plank as grip tightened for escape – her new bestie, obviously.

For a brief moment Stacey could breathe. With wooden shrapnel piercing on all sides she inhaled God's air, sweet, cool, and calm. Her chest loosened, and her lips curled upward: someone was near, in the forest with her, and as a team they would escape. However, with each rap for traction the ground shook, with it the idea of friendly inclusion: how could such a tiny hand cause such cataclysm?

Stacey's instincts prepped for the worst once again, a pound of the chest screaming for retreat. She fought against her own wits, fought for blind faith that everything would be okay, alas her lungs and heart retreated, constricted, making air and blood circulation scarce, yet again, proving that all was *not* right on an instinctual level.

"Help me," whispered the sweetest voice buried deep, below the door.

Stacey's fear disappeared: the door didn't hold a monster; no, it held a girl in need of help! New dexterity posed as she valiantly ran to aid, the idea of warm hugs extinguishing cold chills revitalizing her wits. She grabbed the distraught limb and pulled toward freedom.

Every muscle in Stacey's body ached, joints popped loud and fierce, yet she still could not free her new friend. The tiny hand anchored by the weight of the world, seemingly. Nonetheless, she attempted to free the girl from the hellish pit – that she, herself refused to gaze. She pulled; a few times her grip slipped, and she fell hard, on her ass and elbows. But adrenaline and willpower picked her up each time, and she returned to her task. She would free the cellar dweller…

Even if it caused her slight discomfort.

But once the second arm reached for the surface, Stacey was rendered useless.

Stacey fell backward, for the sixth time to be exact, the release of weight catapulting her onto ass with greater force than before. This time the collision caused enough pain for her to release an audible – *fuck*. Perhaps the pain was only so intense because of the repeated assault, but she was sure skin was broken, and possibly her tailbone was cracked. The event had evolved past *slight discomfort*. However, no sooner than she began caressing her sore hams, the pain was replaced—yet again—with concentrated fear. Pain at her nerve-endings gave way to her heart pounded against her rib cage. Her sore ass retracted soothing request and instead scooted back against the hard ground. No care for further injury, only escape. A girlish figure slithered out of the cellar, resembling a deadly snake protruding a hellish borrow. Her hands lifted from *butt* cheeks to *face* cheeks, covering her agape mouth, perhaps trying to avoid horror and disbelief from entering like a damned fly.

The *girl* from within the cellar door, was no girl at all, she realized that now. Instead, Stacey was faced with a ghoulish creature – possibly a girl, at one point. Its skin was in a state of decay, hanging off the muscle, innards visible. Black ooze dripped from each wound and fell to the ground producing a faint sizzle. Its face: sunken, pruned from lack of moisture, and bared monstrous gashes. But no blood, other than the ooze. Demon's blood? Instead, porcelain bone gleamed from beneath the surface. A putrid, toxic cloud consumed the air surrounding the creature.

Stacey stifled back vomit, as the deathly odor filled her lungs, but couldn't stifle the tears filling her eyes from the horrific sight. She didn't wait for permission to squirm away from the creature—perhaps instinct should have taken the wheel hours ago.

The creature's eyes gazed, laser pointed on Stacey. She attempted to avoid contact, afraid of turning to stone, or being tranced into submission. Mostly, she avoided eye-contact out of disgust and protocol. Since childhood she was taught to close her eyes, not to look at monsters in movies, not to give them validation. If only it had worked with Chris, then she would be able to believe its successfulness in this instance. Unfortunately, regardless of eye contact the ghoulish creature *was* real, and whispered, "help me," directly into Stacey's ears like a monster would be able—her *flight* sense heightened.

Enough fucking around had transpired. Enough praying and internal debate about validity had owned Stacey's wits. Now, was the time for pure fear and subsequent retreat. She rolled over, back toward the girl and dug her hands deep in the dirt for traction; she started slow but picked up speed quickly. Should she have stood to run? No, she wouldn't trip like some horror flick bimbo, she stayed her course, ignoring the scrapes and multiple heart attaches she surely had. She would live long enough for a doctor to make proper notoriety of studying her new and profound ability to overcome physical pain and shock.

Stacey adjusted to the situation, if she was going to survive she would need to gain speed. Each advance her nemesis made shook the ground. Mixing the terrain with the quakes, her chances of successfully fleeing while upright, seemed feeble. But, she was getting tired and her palms were giving up the fight as blood stained the ground. So, she overcame the shaking ground and found footing. She had to run, she had to put greater distance between herself and the creature – simple horror tactics; running *is* faster than crawling.

A small path appeared, as if from thin air, delivered for Stacey's escape. She took haste, ran through the opening. She ran till her legs entered muscle memory and moved forward on autopilot. In little time she was far enough ahead that the trembling ground faded to nothing more than a hyperbole—perhaps she imagined it all to begin with. Stacey's pounding heart lightened – her rib cage thankful – and *autopilot* switched off when she came across her belongs on the forest floor. Never before had a girl been as happy to find her bag. She was going the right way, she had to be. How else did she find her bag? An intense urge to double her courage with liquid substance erupted. She scanned for the beast, quickly, to ensure there was time. She opened her bag and retrieved the bottle of whiskey for a couple swigs, taking the edge off would aid escape, obviously.

The whiskey hit her tongue and throat with such fire. A fire she hated a lifetime ago, but now couldn't live without. A taste she needed to bury the horrors of her *new* life. But the booze took hold of her wits more so than usual, and faster. With only a few swigs her head lightened, and the forest spun.

"None of this SHIT is real," she laughed, taunting the forest. Again, the forest resembled a friendly place, a dark place she could erupt without repercussion. In an instant the bugs disappeared, and furry creatures whisked about without care of Stacey. Hell, for a moment she thought she caught sight of the overgrown pig, now in the thralls of fornication – guess it was a girl pig.

Stacey shrugged and sighed deep at the nights adventures. She finished off the bottle and held it out like a divine compass. After a couple eyes-shut spins, she stopped and embarked on her new direction of travel, confident in the Whiskey God's wisdom. She marched on, whistling with little care of the world and with no care for an imaginary goo-girl crawling around.

"Now, where is that fucker at? Come out, Chris, I'm here to fuck *your* world up!"

Funny thing about cocky people: they tend to look up, snubbed nose toward the world in their travels, something completely against personal safety in a forest. Not to mention the Widow Forest. Stacey did exactly that: she puffed her chest, turned nose to the sky and marched toward Chris – or so she thought. Unfortunately, she turned nose *so* high she tripped over something large on the ground, knocking the wind from her lungs, again. When she rolled over to examine the unworthy, piece of shit, nature incumbent, shock returned as she faced the wretched beast and her senses spiraled, fear wasn't even apparent for several moments as she aligned all the senses and factors – it caught up, very horror movie-like, Jason like. This time the two were inches from each other. The beast stared into Stacey's eyes whispering, again, "Help me."

"That voice," Stacey whispered through cracked vocals and tearful eyes, not to the beast, but to herself in hopes of sparking memory. Each hair on her body erected in warning – no ignoring biological response this time.

She had heard that voice before. And like a smack to a faulty computer, her brain rebooted, flashing all the truths in front of her eyes. Wiping the doubt of her own wickedness. It was the voice traveling on the wind the night before. The voice she decided was her imagination was now teamed with a doomed creature less than two-feet away. Never before had Stacey been face to face with a consequence of this magnitude. Her internal circuits shorted, she went passed fight and flight, and stopped at freeze, with only tears of confusion streaming down her face.

Stacey froze, as did the ghoulish girl. She shuffled closer, slowly to avoid panic and whispered, "I am so sorry," through tear-filled eyes. She scooted *even* closer, the smell and sight seeming to come from her own retched soul – it smelled like home, now – her soul was stuck inside that ghoulish figure, and maybe, just maybe, she could get it back. The wretched sight before her, was nothing more than a visual result of what she had become. She wanted to correct it, she wanted to regain an ounce of her former self. Her goodness, or the last shred of it, trapped beneath the wrenched body, and she wanted it back.

The beast reached a hand out, toward Stacey, slow-and-calm.

Stacey sat, watching the small, decaying hand move closer. Hoping it was the hand of grace, the hand of forgiveness she didn't dare avoid its plan. She watched it make final descent, in angelic fashion, swaying lightly downward resembling the movement of a feather on the wind. However, the visual and physical of this event were far from complimentary: the hand landed, resting on Stacey's ankle.

l

Stacey screamed in agony. The small, frail hand gently placed on her ankle, felt like a metric-fuck-ton. A loud *pop* pierced the silence and her bones cracked, the sounds attacked her senses from out and within, coinciding with the pain and grinding that sent her nervous system into hyperdrive; her heart-rate reached a new high for the evening and every nerve in her body screamed for retreat. She pulled away, but the weight was too much, her leg stretched like a rubber band as she tried to escape the weight that kept her stationary. Stacey flailed for release, fuck a leg. She could survive without it, surly it was dead anyways, she simply needed to go home. She called out for Daddy to rescue her. She flung her remaining limbs about, ignoring the pain of cuts and scraps against natures floor in attempt to subside the truly horrific pain her trapped leg was under.

Between Stacey's screams the ghoulish girl whispered, "Help me," over, and over, spraying black ooze, a thick substance like tar that smelled of death and moved about like slugs with needles for tendrils across Stacey's being.

Stacey watched, helplessly as the beast raised its other arm and slowly placed it on her free, flailing leg. Again, the bones splintered, blood ran to the ground. Her bones protruded from skin – Mother Nature quickly absorbed Stacey's blood, utilizing her essence for the circle-of-life, and removing evidence of her turmoil.

Stacey frantically pulled, trying to escape the weight, with even less success as both legs were destroyed and detained. How could this be real? With physical command of her own body restricted, she retreated into her mind attempting to discredit the events. Only in a world where God existed could such an event transpire, but in that case why would God let this happen to her? No, this couldn't be real, she wouldn't – couldn't – believe her life would end like that of horror movies.

"Please, please, stop! Please, you're killing me!" Stacey screamed. If the girl wouldn't listen, perhaps God would. He had to know in her heart that she was sorry and was worthy of forgiveness.

The ghoulish girl remained silent and lifted her first hand and extended further up Stacey's body, placing it on Stacey's stomach. Stacey's stomach depressed and released blood like a squeezed sponge – her life essence gushed onto the ground like a broken water main. The delicate hand shattered her spine paralyzingly the lower extremities in-tow with excruciating pain. The girl used the posture to drag her body on top of Stacey. Her thin body, like a steamroller, smashing all of the bones Stacey's feet and legs in the process.

"HELP ME! SOMEONE, PLEASE HELP ME!" Stacey screamed to forest walls.

The ghoulish face twisted, angrily: eyes bulged and exploded; lips ripped away at the seams producing a wicked smile and dislodged jaw; the skull splintered and bulged spaying ooze, leaving fragments resembling spikes on the *new* face. And her hands, her hands balled into Stacey's flesh crumpling skin and matter as if nothing more than a leaf of paper. She picked up speed grunting and ripping away at Stacey with each stroke. Her body pushed all Stacey's innards upward treating her like a damned tube of toothpaste.

Stacey's screams became garbled moans as she choked on her own blood and bile.

The beast was nearing Stacey's screaming face, where she placed a delicate finger above Stacey's lips, without an ounce of weight, signally a request for silence.

Stacey slowed her screaming to a dull whimper between breaths and mouthfuls of blood. Face-to-face with a twisted, angry beast instead of a sad broken girl. She yearned for the nightmare to end, for death to release her from the horrific scene.

Stacey whispered, again, "please, help me." Again, not to the beast, but to God, in hopes of mercy.

The dead girl enthralled in anger, replied, "NO BITCH, HELP ME!" She dropped her entire – tiny in frame, but heavy in woe – body onto Stacey.

Stacey's blood littered the ground faster than nature could absorb leaving a trail of viscera as she was trailed underneath the beast. She should have been dead, she knew that. But instead she still felt life in her collapsed chest. Her body was broken, but her soul was condemned inside.

The dead girl crawled, dragging Stacey, toward the Cellar Door that appeared from the darkness. She peered into the opening and called out, "Someone, please help us." She put one hand in front of the other and began descent into the darkness.

Stacey shook her head lightly in contest: *us?* The entire night skipped her mind as this one word repeated. What did it mean? Was she a victim like the ghoulish girl? Who could help them at this point in the pits below. She softly shook her head – or perhaps her damaged body simply reacted to movement along the rocky path. But either way, Stacey was taking a trip, leaving town as she wanted, never to be seen or heard from again. Leaving behind only the memory of Daddy's *Little One*, the memory of a *good girl*.

Chris

"Babe I know you saw the sign. I don't want to go into the damn woods! Let's just go back to my house and watch a movie, okay?"

The sound of Sarah's infant-like voice penetrated Chris's mind like shards of glass. Luckily, he was walking ahead of her, giving him the ability to mock her without her knowing his insult. Regardless of his silence, he knew he trained her well; she was too stupid to disobey his lead. He let her continue about the creepy spirit inside the forest, about nothing ever being the same inside the forest, about leaving the forest and not having to eat bugs for sustenance. A twisted smile formed, she couldn't see anyway. She had no idea that the only thing she would be eating in the forest, was his throbbing prick. Hell, he would even give her a preemptive slap to the fucking mouth to make sure she didn't get any crazy ideas, like biting or fighting. She was equally hot and annoying, and payment was due for his façade.

"Look I don't really care what you do but I'm going in," Chris commanded, matter-of-factly. "I've done this so many times, babe, you don't need to worry."

But – truthfully – he hadn't, and yes, she was correct to be worried. Not of the forest, no, her nerves should be screaming for retreat because he was going to torment and ravish her body till she wished he would kill her. Then, and only then, could he be happy with the journey required to corner this piece of meat. Chris chuckled again, louder this time. The sign warning all not to enter should be changed to warn young cunts not to enter *with him*. But her obvious disregard for warning signs would be his reward.

Thus, the two travelled into the forest's grasp. Their wits warned, for a brief moment, of the horror ahead with a sharp pain to the gut. But both continued, focused more on personal pleasure than personal safety: Chris, focused on the pleasure of rape and torture, Sarah on the idea of a moonlit adventure with her love – something each could tell offspring years later. They took comfort in each other for a moment to recover from biological warning by grasping hands and sharing a tender kiss. Oblivious to the depth at which they traveled away from safety. Or maybe it was nature shrouding the area making travel seem short, either way they moved far from safety. The entrance, or rather, the exit to their safety disappeared. Bottom line, no amount of *breadcrumbs* could return them to safety.

Sarah was the first to notice the world had changed around them. As critters scurried about behind nights shroud the hairs on her body stood erect, which excited Chris, making his prick erect. He wanted to extend thanks, with every step, to: spiders, ants, or worse of all A FUCKING SKUNK, attacking her legs. With each sound of nature's movement culprit evolved into something worse. Honestly, it was as if the forest was in-tune with his plan and was offering natural foreplay for his desires.

"Chris, please stop." She demanded.

"Hun, we can't just stop. Then the creepy-fucking-crawlies will touch that sexy body of yours and I won't be able to stop your screams." Chris replied – sweetly?

"Chris, I said, STOP!" Sarah screamed.

She never questioned him with a raised tone, if he didn't turn on the charm then his plan would surely be fucked. So, he stopped.

His body yearned to ask her a giant helping of *WTF* but he noticed her fear. That and the finger up to her lips to *shush,* and the tears traveling down her gorgeous cheeks. Delicious tears that should belong to him, but time hadn't come for him to attack yet, no matter how *hard* he was. Once they were deep enough into the forest he would rip her clothes off and fuck her, hopefully against her will, hard-and-loud. Away from any decent form of humanity. Deep enough in the woods for them to behave as man and woman were meant: him, strong and dominate. She, weak and submissive.

He wanted tears, and for her to scream for help, but he had to hold back. He wasn't sure if they were deep enough, yet. And he wasn't going to let a stupid cunt like Sarah get away – not after months of *boyfriending.*

So, he obliged to her request and *shut-the-fuck-up*, like a gentlemen.

The night concealed any true visual investigation, but scarier: it also concealed any sound: Chris finally understood why Sarah looked terrified. He wasn't scared, but he knew why she was, there was no sound coming from the surroundings. Perhaps everything was holding fast, enjoying the show, he thought. Hoping to catch the feral act he planned to unleash.

Darkness filled their lungs with fear as they stood still. Their bodies constricted, naturally trying to expel the unwanted intruder. Chills followed, coupled with quickened breath and uncontrollable chattering of teeth. Sarah finally broke stillness, broke silence, and lunged toward Chris, wrapping her arms around his neck.

"Please take me home, I'm so scared." She whispered, softly into his ear.

"The only way out is through, Sarah," Chris lied. "That's how this place works, we just keep going straight and come out the other end. I promise we're close, okay? Just hold my hand and keep moving."

He was a professional douche – *Island Splash* scent with long lasting results. In not much more than one year he had perfected his ability to use his boyish good looks and charm in unison with asshole(ish) intention.

Chris ecstatically led this way and that, around trees and over small streams of water, his hand trembling, either from nearing climax or the nights chill, he couldn't be sure.

Excitement won the verdict due to a rock-hard *gavel*.

Sarah followed like a young child grasping at daddy's shirt through a crowd. "Chris, slow down. I can't remember which way is out anymore." She pleaded.

A demonic laugh filled the space between Chris's ears. She couldn't be so stupid, could she? The presence of humankind was long gone. He would be her dominator soon enough – her one true God.

"Quit thinking so much. I know where we are." He said – a lie. For a single heartbeat that fact entered his thoughts but his mission bitchslapped any common sense from his mind. He reset his wits with a simply shake-of-the-head.

Chris was finally content with their seclusion. Surely when he announced, "*scream if you want bitch, no one will hear you,*" it would be true. So, he halted. In the same spot Sarah initially stopped for a moment of silence, unbeknownst to Chris – he failed to comprehend such. No, instead of realizing he was a mouse on a treadmill, he examined the state of his efforts' prize: Sarah.

Chris swelled with pride as Sarah lost composer, frantically searching left, then right, forcing long, deep breaths and swelling her ample milk bags. Cold beads of sweat streaming down her slender neck and disappearing between the fleshy mountains, tempting him to follow – fear was his greatest aphrodisiac.

He appreciated her state, giving him plenty of time to get his castration-worthy plan in order. It had to be perfect, if he was lucky she might even go home and kill herself. If he did a good enough job, that would be *tug* worth for months. Plus, he wouldn't need to worry about any tattling.

Teenage deductive reasoning, meet adult, douchey predator yearnings.

Simply put: Fucktard.

Chris savored her fear. It was delicious, it was power. It was *his* power. But something over her shoulder wiped the smile from his face.

Between several trees in the distance was a faint gleam. Was it a flashlight? He couldn't properly focus on his task if, by some small chance, someone would witness the act. The light twinkled, almost like a come-hither wink; baiting him to investigate.

"Stay here." He commanded and moved past her. "Or your punishment will be even worse."

Sarah whisper-yelled her confusion, but Chris was already gone – mentally. His focus was consumed by the damned light piercing through his soul, calling-out his actions like a taunt.

Each step through nature's obstacles echoed in his ears. Sarah's whispers mute altogether but he was sure she would remain still. Once he fulfilled his urge of distinguishing the damned gleam he would be able to return focus to his rapey scenario.

That's right, he announced remembering his sole purpose for entering the forest: Sarah. Who cared about some faint light anyway? It was probably nothing more than moonlight bouncing off some unimportant nature *thingy.*

He returned his wits and advance to the *real deal*: Sarah. But she was no where to be found. Surely, he didn't travel more than a few paces away. Therefore, Sarah must have run off, the *bitch* was gone. He surveyed the dark, much like he surveyed his mind when a teacher asked for an answer, little surprise: he came up empty.

"The FUCK, Sarah!? Where are you!?" Chris yelled. Why couldn't *bitches* just get what's coming to them, without making it difficult? Like previously stated:

Fucktard.

Chris spun in circles trying to find some form of a trail, a way Sarah would follow. He did, see something, but not what he was hoping to see: Instead of a chesty damsel with primed asshole ready for the unauthorized docking of his battleship, he was face-to-face with the Cellar Door.

"This can't be it," he whispered to the darkness. And the darkness replied *oh yes it is.*

He jumped, a chill down his spine, raising the hair on his body hoping to evacuate pore and find sanctuary.

He had no idea where the voice came from, he assumed fear was getting the better of him – for once he was right, only not in some figurative way, no, it was besting him, literally.

The Cellar Door was nuzzled in-between a gathering of trees. Its doors old, unappealing and made from weathered pallet wood. Its resting place random and crude. Honestly, it looked fake, as if it was nothing more than a juvenile attempt at a Halloween decoration that was dropped in the meadow to scare those to dumb to investigate.

A small laugh escaped his lips and he broke gaze of the door, and resumed search for Sarah. But his search was hindered more than moment before, the trees thicker hiding any path. In fact, there was but one small opening away from the door, and the trees were so close he couldn't squeeze through. He glanced up, in hope the sky above would calm his nerves, but a web of branches shrouded the sky above.

The fucktard's heart began to race.

He screamed for Sarah to return, to help him. But his screams only reached the trees.

The Cellar Door broke the silence, rattling. Something below wanted release from whatever hellish pit was below.

Chris gaze toward the door hoping it would cease – a skill he learned from a plumber halting ghosts – but alas, Mario failed him. Something wanted out, Chris wanted it to stay in. He crept backwards and pressed against the furthest tree line hoping distance would somehow save him from the act.

The door ceased, and silence demanded attention with an eerie hum, Chris obliged. And with full audience the door shattered, releasing an explosion of light, pieces of the door flying through the air like shrapnel.

Chris covered his eyes from assault. Debris flew about his back as the earth shook beneath his fingers. But the sounds and projectiles tapered as fast as the event began. And slowly, Chris removed face from cover. In as much time as a breath passing he knew it was the worst decision of his life. He could have stayed shrouded from the horrific sight and pretended everything was over. He could have slept, passing time with sweet dreams waiting for sunlight's warm embrace upon his back before blissfully waking. The sun could have extinguished any beasts and illuminated the exit. But none of that would happen, because he looked up. His skin crawled, the content of his bowels evacuated, piss ran down his leg, and his eyes quivered at the sight before him. He couldn't remove his gaze from the sight, the damned sight of pure horror.

Less than *four-hot-bitches-worth-of-space* from Chris stood a ghoulish werewolf foaming at the mouth, teeth exposed through a smile, or snarl – Chris couldn't be sure which. The beast's red eyes pierced through the darkness. Matted black fur blended the beast's form with surrounding darkness. Wolfey must have been at least 7-feet-tall, muscular, with arms made for shredding, and legs made for chasing. However, none of this seemed to invoke fear in Chris. No, he was focused on one thing, and one thing alone.

Wolfey was packing a thick, hard, veiny, foot-long cock. This thing was visibly pulsating it was so hard, the blood rushing through each vein keeping the member erect. Wolfey's cock had a mind of its own, and it was staring, with its one eye, at Chris – and Chris was staring back, in fear.

"You better run, little piggy," Wolfey snarled. The beast spit into its hand and stroked the massive cock. "Because I am coming to hump, and pump, and blow your asshole out!"

Chris raised his hands to wipe the nightmare away. *This can't be fucking happening,* he thought. Regardless of his ability to trust the sight before him, the terror evolved when he realized his hands morphed into giant, man-size hooves. He would go down as the first documented Manbearpig; minus the bear, so Manpig. He was a werepig, and given the fact that there was a MWC (Massive Werewolf Cock) in front of him, he needed to get his tight, pretty, pig ass moving.

The forest parted behind Chris, initiating the chase parameters, he turned piggy-tail and ran. Instinct carried him across the terrain, hooves slamming the soil, in fact, he followed instinct so far he let out a, *SQUEEEEEEEEEE.*

Yup, three little pigs – minus two pigs – and a big thick cock, and no fucking brick house in sight.

Chris could feel Wolfey's eyes – all three – following him. Could sense the erection pulsing at the sight of the pretty pig ass bouncing up-and-down.

"Ready or not, little piggy, here I come." Wolfey exclaimed with a howl. Wolfey dropped to all fours, his member level, tucked against his chest, navigate toward its prey.

Chris pushed his legs hard into the ground and galloped away from the nightmarish beast with as much force as a werepig could. Fuck Sarah, fuck doors and gleaming lights, fuck everything, all that matter was protecting his life – and ass – and leaving the rapey beast in the dust for another to happen upon.

Trees came-and-went like a blur, the less he could identify the better he felt, speed was his friend. The wind felt cold against his skin. *Good*, he thought. He was moving fast. But every part of his body shouldn't've been cold, unless: he no longer had any clothes on. He was just a smooth werepig, naked, running through the Widow Forest. No bother, he couldn't stop, life – and ass – depended on speed, on constant movement. There was *no* way the beast could catch up. Chris got cocky – pun intended – about his evasive piggy abilities, he wasted breath on laughter and insult over his piggy shoulder – guess he was a straw, or stick kind of pig.

"Fuck you, mangy mutt! This is my dream!" Chris screamed. The battle cry cost him a much-needed leap over an oncoming log. Chris tumbled, snout over hoof, and slid to a stop. A warm sensation of blood on his potbelly coupled with a burning pain kept him grounded – forest burn: what a piggy-bitch.

The stumble broke his concentration from the task, at hoof. He lay in the mud – again, pun intended – if he just gained his wits, then the nightmare would disappear, right? It wasn't till two paws straddled his shoulders buried into the ground that his mind connected events: trouble had caught up. He, in-turn, buried his face in the dirt and commanded reality's return. He didn't want to play the nightmarish game any longer.

"*Shhhhhhhh,*" soothed Wolfey, commanding Chris to turn over.

Chris instinctively rolled onto his back, against better judgment: *Why did I do that,* Chris thought. Just like his victims, he instinctively followed the commands of his attacker. Drool dripped to his face and suctioned due to viscosity. Warm precum slowly covered his potbelly from the MWC, shielding his tender hide from natures nip, but also filling his soul with high tended terror.

"That was too easy, Piggy" Wolfey began. "I tell you what, you put the tip in that pretty, piggy mouth, and I'll give you another chance to get away. What do you say?"

Why hadn't Chris woken from this terrible nightmare? The wolf's hot breath smelled of bacon, something Chris used to love, but now feared. He closed his tearful eyes and nodded: yes.

"That's a good, Piggy." Wolfey chuckled.

Chris shimmied down, back scraping the ground, until his head leveled with Wolfey's cock. He was trapped between the massive, cock's head and Wolfey's – which hung down enjoying the show. Why was his doing any of this? He should have run head first into a tree, full speed, at least if he was dead he wouldn't have been face-to-face with the largest, scariest cock the world ever knew. But he didn't, and now his body did what his mind screamed not to: his head lifted from natures core and his mouth fell agape.

The cock's slit erupted.

"Sorry," Wolfey laughed, "all the build-up I guess...you tease."

With the chunky-bitter-salty liquid in his mouth, Chris accepted this was not a dream. A new level of fear captured his wits and he cried out for a savior, for an escape.

Wolfey took advantage of Chris's wails and shoved his cock in the moist suckhole.

The edges of Chris's lips ripped as the cock grew like a balloon in his mouth, a constant stream of cum choking him as well. He fought, trying to capture some air before giving in and swallowing to make room for air intake. Tears of disbelief and moans of sorrow simply made Wolfey more aroused. A never-ending pain, Chris believed. He felt his stomach growing from massive amounts of wolf seed.

After several, all-to-familiar, rapey moans from the wolf, the cock retracted, covered with spit and vomit. Finally, Chris could breathe. His mouth even displayed a slight smile from the ability to breathe again – the small things make life worthwhile.

"Thanks Piggy, now it won't be so hard to ram into that piggy ass...you got me all kinds of lubricated." Wolfey explained. "Now, I am going to count to ten...better run."

Chris didn't even wait for the beast to finish. He rolled over and ran as fast as piggly possible. Tears fled his face, lost in the wind, something he wished to do. Was this punishment for all the girls he raped? No; he just gave the girls what they deserved. This was simply some devil on Earth that knew no bounds.

Still a nasty, stupid, evil...

fucktard.

"Four, Piggy!" The beasts voice echoed from every direction.

How was Chris supposed to escape if the beast was coming from *every* direction?

Chris ran. Well, had been running, but Wolfey's voice penetrated his brain as if inches away. Maybe his *suitor* actions, noble as they were, led him here. Had he just left the girls alone, let someone else give them what they deserved, he wouldn't be having such a painful and unnecessary experience.

"Eight, Piggy!" Wolfey announced; voice echoing off the trees.

The trees around Chris grew, bigger, and bigger as his stride seemed to decrease, smaller, and smaller. He turned his head, for just one second, to see how far he had traveled, and the beast standing in front of the Cellar Door. The door that should have been miles away.

"How the fuck am I back here?" The fresh scent of sap smashed against Chris's snout. Or more accurately, he smacked into a tree covered in sap – he always had an issue understanding whom attacked whom. Fuck the pain, he had more pressing issues. For instance, being stuck, yet again, in a circle of trees around the Cellar Door. Face-to-face with a much larger wolf, a much larger cock with equally larger, throbbing veins.

Chris wanted to run, wanted to scream, but an uncontrollable shake left him lying on the ground in convulsions. His eyes, unable to cry any longer, simply pleaded for retreat, for one more chance at escape. But his voice was the only thing left in his arsenal that could possible gain aid. He announced to the heavens his need for a savior. But all that came out was:

"SQUEEEEEEEEEE!"

Chris executed a quick computation of *two-and-two* and exposed *four*: he had transformed into an *actual* pig. No sooner than he made the determination, he was filled with an uncontrollable urge to trot away rather than dissect imaginary from reality. He ran in circles – like pigs do – searching for escape, as traumatic squeals fell from his piggy lips.

"Ten...little piggy." Wolfey Concluded, towering the potbelly pig. He picked up his piggy prize with firm grip.

Chris squirmed but the grip was so tight. He couldn't do anything but hope for it to end soon. For the threat to become bored and leave. A threat Chris knew all too well, yet, now from a terrifying vantage.

Wolfey moaned, slowly penetrating the squealing asshole's asshole. The head announced insertion – *pop*. The shaft followed like a freight train into a dark tunnel.

Chris had long forgotten how to express dismay, with each pounding he face simply contorted: his tears, dried up, his screams, died out. He simply wanted to get away, he wanted to wake up, he wanted this to be nothing more than a nightmare. A nightmare that grew with each passing second; the cock growing in length and girth tearing his backside.

A thundering howl signaled each time Wolfey climaxed – each time his piggy slave regurgitated a river of cum to the forest floor.

The beast turned toward the cellar door, still pumping and carefully keeping stride. Hovering its cock over the hole, Wolfey gave his piggy companion front row view of the absolute void below. The door was not the end of the journey, yet, the beginning with no hope for a happy ending – pun intended – for Chris. Pain from behind seemed less horrific to the idea of entering hell's pit and becoming a piggy sex doll for all time.

"Little pig, little pig...." Wolfey began, "LET ME IN!"

His claws dug deep into Piggy Chris's sides. Chris opened mouth wide to yell, but the pain of being penetrated by fingers left him without voice. The probes punctured his skin, organs, and shattered ribs. Chris was fading, the loss of blood and pain was too great.

The beast achieved the desired leverage and grip to give it his all, to give the little piggy what it wanted – whether Chris asked or not. He rammed harder, faster, tracking Chris's body over the void then against bristle wolf bush, over-and-over.

The beast's cock finally outgrew the entirety of Chris's piggy body, exiting the snout, making a pork kabob. Wolfey dropped its hands in rest leaving Chris hung off the erection, convulsing about the rod for a moment before dangling, dead, as if a cock ring, of sorts.

"Well, piggy, time to go home." Wolfey concluded. Walking down the stairs, into the darkness. "I need a rest, so when you wake up we can play again."

The door slammed shut, and once again was hidden by the moss and growth of Widow Forest.

Sarah woke the next morning in her bed swearing she was with Chris the night before and that the forest took him. Her parents assured she was home the whole night. Chris was missing, and it was only normal that his current girlfriend be upset. But her mom and dad wouldn't hear of such nonsense tales: Widow Forest was legend, not truth.

Tony

The crisp night air nipped at Tony's face, snot and tears became icy chapping his skin. With each wipe of his face the pain grew. Shelter of any kind would have been welcomed, giving him shelter from the brutality of weather. However, sirens in the distance raised his skin with prickled bumps, prompting immediate seclusion, and with no modern structure in sight, he moved past the sign at the edge of Widow Forest. Even cops believed in the urban legend, so he would surely be able to hide within, enduring the weather was an easy price to pay for escape.

Tony, a young 17-year-old boy with freckled, pasty-white skin – wrapping large muscles – and curly red hair, never believed he would be running from the police; his looks typically made him the victim.

As he squeezed past trunks of large trees and tackled thick brush he whispered to the wind about his accomplishments and the unfair situation: why was *he* a target? He was an all-around *great* kid. Star of the football team and a straight 'A' student, he even volunteered, his parents believed it strengthened strong morals and character.

He travelled deeper into the forest, far enough from the road, far enough from passing ears. He spoke aloud of injustice, a shallow attempt at convincing himself of a worldly wrongdoing. Surely he was a better person than most in the world, especially anyone in that damned town, so judgment would not be passed on him – not by the likes of *them.*

"So I made some mistakes, I've made up for that shit," Tony explained. "And I am a kid. It isn't my fault." He plead to Mother Nature, but no calming response returned for his testimony. Or so he believed; a large, icy gust of wind momentarily crippled his movement – he didn't catch the hint.

So he bullied some kids, maybe they shouldn't have been such losers. Yeah, he wasn't the most respectable kid to adults, but he was surely smarter and *better* than them. Good behavior and moral conduct was reserved for the hard working and deserving.

For years, he was teased for being a scrawny redhead with ghostly white skin and lack of a soul; did he complain? No. Did he bitch to adults or cry when kids pushed him around or neglected his presence? No. Hell, he didn't even hold it against Mr. Corrin, the teacher that witnessed him receive a hefty beating in middle school. Because Tony wasn't a loser. Instead he worked hard and became better than everyone around him.

He vowed never again to be the weakest or *dumbest* person. He simply gave those whom were the weakest and dumbest a hard time to initiate drive and evolution. He wasn't a *true* bully, he detested bullies. But others needed a way out of Loserville and it was his service to society to drive the bus.

But now he had to hide in a damned forest, all because of Scott. Surely he bitched and cried to his parents about the beating Tony delivered the day before. Where others chose to ignore Scott and his crazy actions, Tony took it upon himself to correct the situation.

With all the disappearances lately, and people – adult and kid alike – coming up injured, surely Tony's *minor* infraction was making him prime suspect. Just another way the world was full of unintelligent fucktards. He hadn't done anything to any of those people. His victims could be called to the stand, could explain the brutal therapy Tony bestowed, because all were alive, from this lifetime.

"None of those losers could make it this far into the woods," He whispered matter-of-factly. Too bad his body didn't believe the words. Instead his wits excited while his skin tightened. His teeth clenched, locked even, to stop the chattering. His balls shriveled into a painful prune like state. But he wouldn't listen to his body, he simply grabbed at his crotch and tugged.

His father always said; *only the opinions of educated and, or hardworking people mattered.* Tony was both, and he didn't have time or patience for those who weren't. Even his younger sister didn't display the traits father laid out like commandments. Maybe that was why she died. Not that he had anything to do with it, a higher power decided her fate – one he understood and welcomed.

Tony's thoughts echoed in the forest as if screams; surrounding silence carried his notions through web of trees and darkness. He alternated between his inner and outer voices, but both echoed through his ears, a commanding voice he couldn't escape.

The forest was listening, something Tony didn't take into account as he laid his life out to the world. From beyond his feet and sight the shrubs, bugs, and critters came, listening to his story. The forest came alive, with his rant. A show secluded by the darkness and harrowing growth of Widow Forest. Making sure there was plenty of space between them and he, as to not encounter the same fate by association; yet, close enough to watch yet another wicked soul meet justice.

The darkness and silence took hold of his wits, his mind went blank, filled with the darkest void, stopping him dead in his tracks. Moments ago, the forest path was nothing more than harrowing, but in an instance, had become tormenting. The surrounding air warmed, seemingly instant. His muscles relaxed stopping his jitters and calming nerves. He sat against a tree to rest. The warmth covered his body, massaging his legs; when did they become sore? How far had he walked? No matter, the warmth and rest disposed of fear and anxiety. A deep breath filled his lungs with warm air and his fears dissipated that much more.

He buried his face in his hands, attempting to reset his situation, hoping to make sense of the emotional onslaught; but instead, he simply cried. Sure, tears escaped his eyes over the years, but this was different.

He bellowed. He sobbed. He asked…

Why?

He let go of everything and was carried back to a vulnerable place from his past. Mother nature was coddling him, wrapping him in a warm embrace. It was only proper that he open up, that he release the tension, guilt, and fear onto her bosom.

A whisper carried on the wind tore Tony from his self-deprecation. His ears sharpened enough to produce a twitch; trying to catch the whisper. He pulled up to his feet. The voice was long gone mere seconds after announcement, but his ears led him deeper into the forest to investigate.

He called out to the darkness with less effort than a whisper: *hello*. No response. He continued his travels, but with a new mission: finding his company. Something about being alone with Mother Nature, nestled in the eerie, calm darkness induced a primal yearning for human presence. Hell, anyone in this forest was brave enough to be considered his equal, too long had people plagued the minds of this small town with lies about demons, judgement, and death in relation to this damned forest. Eerie as it was, there was no need for such lies, or fears...obviously.

The foliage thickened around him with each step. Stride after stride, Tony continued, his legs disregarding the situational changes. Ignoring the need for pause. Instead his feet cycled forward to a silent cadence, without Tony's approval.

"Hello? Do you need help? You seem lost."

Who the fuck; Tony thought. His legs agreed to pause, attempting silence for investigation: nothing.

His hands had to lead the way as moonlight escaped sight beneath the shroud of treetops. As if situations weren't intense enough, a *creepy-crawly* bit his leg: he reached down to dole out punishment. Timing played perfect, as Tony swatted for the terrorist attached to his lower extremity a scream erupted, breaking silence. For a moment he thought it came from the insect; absurd – it came from behind the cascade of darkness beyond Tony's eyes. Before the last echo disappeared, he answered by way of full sprint – not too smart in the dark, and from a kneeling position.

Oh, how the mighty fall. Tony stumbled and without ability to recover fell forward through branches and bushes. Natures tight womb spit him out into a lush, green clearing. The moonlight, bright and vibrant, drenched the scene; Tony could have counted each perfect blade of grass, if so desired, regardless of the midnight hour. The sight was calming to the senses – Perhaps search for the *Wizard* could wait till after a nice nap.

His body welcomed the gentle light pouring over lush green growth of grass and moss, his heart slowed. Life wasn't so bad. The natural, minty scent that filled the air cleared his nasal passage. Since birth sweet smells partnered happiness; the situation was improving.

In as many moments as it took for his body to calm, the stress of his situation reignited, like a damned lighter in the hands of a pyro. In the distance, protruding from the meadow floor lay a door. And without understanding why, he ceased his pursuit for the voice-on-the-wind and, instead, answered a primal call for investigation, investigation of a door...*the* door. An investigation that was antonymous to the action for which his body was *screaming*: to neglect, overlook, leave alone, forget; or in a word: *run.*

"No fucking way," He whispered wiping his eyes; surely, tears and fears played culprit for the surreal image before his weary eyes.

Tony answered an Otherly command to advance toward the door. This was wrong...stupid...fucked. But he continued travel, shaking his head through travel: his only way to contest action. Asking himself; *why?* A common occurrence, as of late.

His body screamed with each step of his misunderstanding of the events: His legs trembled to the point of buckle; his hands twitched as he picked off dead and live skin alike from fingertips. As a last resort, his entire respiratory system banded together in futile effort, suffocating him, hoping that conscious effort to capture breath would cancel his pursuit. But alas, in all his *supreme* wisdom and *unchallenged* intelligence, Tony was amiss to the most basic bodily warnings. And, he pushed through, with the door in sight.

He stood above the door, sweat beading and running down his face and arms.

Heat radiated from the door, blasting Tony's skin in waves like an oven door opening and closing.

Movement on the edge of the woods caught Tony's eye: a giant pig ran by, behind the wall of trees; he was barely able to make it out, but he did – or so he thought, since pigs weren't normal in the area. And the momentary lapse of concentration was enough for the situation to change without notice.

"What the fuck is going on?" Tony mouthed, the door a distant priority as a violent squeal rang in his ears from every direction. Surely the pig had met its demise; *good riddance,* he thought, *pigs are filthy animals.*

The pig required more investigation than some weathered door. He walked toward the tree line; maybe it was the pig he heard all along.

But the pig was long gone; or at least noise of such, so Tony returned to perked ears – investigating silence.

Sounds of squeaky hinges in motion broke the silence, his attention sparked, the sound attached to his spine with an icy-chill, shaking him to the core.

His mind told him to run, or pleaded, really: he didn't listen, he never listened. It wanted escape, from the poor decisions, from solidarity, and to welcome social punishment; however, his body ignored instinct and turned around.

The door swung open with monstrous force, a crimson, red glow escaped from below reaching toward the heavens, pin-pointing the location for the horrors to come.

Tony swallowed the fear and regained control of his feet, control was what he needed. Control of his mind, his limbs, and ultimately his fate. So, he took that first step backward. One that would start the momentum needed to unfuck his situation. But alas, when tiny hands grabbed for the surface – too many to discern – his limbs returned to a frozen state, the fear clawed back up his throat, gagging him all the way, and his mind was gone, gone from his control.

"This isn't happening," he exclaimed mouth agape and body trembling full of fear.

One-by-one, the tiny hands pulled tiny bodies to the surface. Correction: tiny *doll* hands pulled tiny *doll* bodies to the surface. Some were rag-dolls, some porcelain, others plastic and cloth. All stood two-to-three feet tall. Each with a blank, generic face, except for the mouth. Each smiled wide exposing large, serrated blades for teeth. The dolls opened-and-closed their mouths repeatedly; filling the air with a hungry smacking noise coupled with metal clanking. They stood in front of the doors, waiting for something – or someone, like dogs on a leash. Staring at Tony like a raw steak, salivating at the delicacy, patiently waiting for command.

Tony sidestepped, left, then right; the dolls meeting his stride with equal advance. However, the creepy little mob never overran, instead simply mirrored his movements, never closing the gap. Tony and the dolls were in a dance, lead-and-follow, but another set of hands reached for the ground from whatever Hell below, consuming the attention of the dolls and Tony.

These hands, dirty and disfigured, but human, pulled up a young girl's body. Tony watched, in awe, as she escaped – what he could only assume was the pits of hell. The tiny dolls, with their sadistically wide grins, full of razor blade teeth, no longer held his attention. Not even as they shrieked and rolled about on the ground around the girl, around their master? Honestly, the only shred of mental power he held for them, was that he needed to teach them to man-up – how could these grotesque little demon-dolls follow the direction of some tiny, girl? If Tony possessed a fearful trait, as they did, he would rule the world – or at least, his world. Nonetheless, she captivated him, and held his attention: She stood, taller than the surrounding demon-dolls, pleased with their joyful trotting. Tony was nothing more than a spectator, but she gave him a devilish smirk; her demon pets echoed the expression, snapping to, and mimicking their leader. He was no longer a spectator, he was the main event.

"Hi Tony," the girl whispered, but several voices cascaded toward his ears. The dolls continued their mimicking act, even through dialogue.

"This can't be happening; you're dead." Tony replied. "This isn't real. None of this is real," Tony continued, convincing himself that there was a lack of validity in the predicament. He met his opposition, fake as it was, toe-to-toe as he had done his whole life. He took one step, then two toward the mob. The dolls snarled and postured for attack. But he paid them no mind, he wouldn't be terrorized by such childish fears, ghosts and demon-dolls were things a crazy person would believe in – things *Scott* would believe in, and Tony was definitely smarter than *that* shitbrick.

There is a lot of good behind self-confidence. But Tony took it to an unsafe place. Nothing new. The kids that weren't smart enough to avoid him at school typically ended up with bruises and complexes due to his self-confidence, and his self-righteousness. The main focus of his attention, Scott, knew this fact more than others. Tony would kick the crazy out of Scott by way of punishment and belittlement or kill him trying. Like the time Scott as in the bathroom, talking to himself, about how he wished he wasn't crazy, wasn't in high school with an imaginary friend that no one else believed in. So, Tony helped him, stripped him naked and duct taped his nuts to his leg. And guess what? There was no imaginary friend that stopped it, surely Scott would get the hint.

Tony was always sure of his actions. He was smart and hardworking. He was of sound mind and body. And the creepy – fake – bitch before him, and her minions, could fuck off. Something he was more than willing to help them do, so he shoved the freaky cunt toward her hole. Hoping to launch her back, from which she came.

But...

She didn't move. Tony shoved with all his might, and she didn't move. The dolls laughed, the *girl* laughed. Unacceptable. Tony created space, decided to ram the bitch. He charged forward, giving a loud yell for effect, but the girl stood her ground.

Their bodies collided, and Tony fell back onto the ground. Hitting the ground hurt less than the collision, but both hurt like the first no pads tackle. His shoulder was aching, and his elbow was bleeding. The warm blood soothed his cold skin, but the burn forced a grimace. He needed time to regain composure, to understand how something so obviously fake was able to dismantle his reality.

He needed *too* much time…

The dolls rushed over, their tiny feet pattering faster than he could follow. Tony tried standing, but tiny hands held him, pinned to the ground. No wonder Andy Barclay and an entire slew of adults couldn't simple hold down a possessed doll: the fuckers were strong.

The dolls, dressed in their bright, tattered sundresses, held Tony to the ground. He squirmed, trying to wiggle free with every once of his being, but their plastic and cloth limbs clamped him to the ground without an ounce of visible effort. The earth rumbled beneath Tony, and the hard ground he clawed at for leverage softened, into mud.

The dolls sank into the soil, all that was left above ground were hands and heads – demonic cabbage patch kids. One-by-one the dolls released their hands, but the relief wouldn't last long. The moonlight beamed on each saturated smirk.

The crop of dolls screamed out for flesh and blood, feeding their urge on Tony's being. They sunk the daggers into his flesh, holding him ridged to the ground.

Tony twisted his body, pushing the pain from his mind in attempt to escape. But the dolls effortlessly bit harder like tiny pit bull puppies. Tony pushed, and pulled harder, angry at how easy the dolls made his capture seem. The taunting hurt more than each gash, his emotion gushing out like the blood from his flesh. The incisions set his nerves on fire, reality sank in as the blood ran, warm, down his body from each point of contact. His essence pooling under his extremities, released to the elements, never to return.

The ghastly girl chuckled. Her skin, weathered and scarred, held tight against her bones from a lack of mass. But even still, she chuckled, as if her dreams were coming true, as if there was no wrong in the world, in her world – she came to bring hell to his. She walked around Tony's bound body, never breaking Tony's gaze; she pushed on the heads of her pets along the traveling inspection: Tony's screams worsened with each addition of pressure.

"Please Vicky, you're my sister!" Tony pleaded with every once of his being, he believed this to be his sister, believed what his eyes feared. And as so, she couldn't take pleasure in his pain, or shouldn't. He couldn't hide his fear, his pain, nor did he want to, so he pleaded again, and again, each time the quiver in his voice increased, his body became uncontrollable, convulsing from the deepest pit of his soul.

Vicky dropped to her knees and kissed Tony's forehead. "I was your sister, until you killed me."

"You teased me, you were the bad one. I was only a kid!" Tony explained, spilling his *truths* into the air.

Vicky stood, peering over Tony, her feeble body seeming reminiscent of a giant.

Tony never felt *so* small in his life.

"We were a year apart, Tony. Don't be dramatic. I never hurt you. We teased each other the way all siblings do," Vicky started, her unwavering stare pierced through his lies, exposing the truth, even to him. "Doesn't matter, you killed me. All because you felt entitled. Because you felt like the world owed you something. Because you cared more about yourself than anything, even me; your sister. And no one every figured it out. Then what did you do?"

Tony shook his head frantically. "I got better. I'm a *good* person, Vicky!"

Vicky laughed.

The shriek pierced Tony's ears and travelled to his bladder – which, coincidently, released its contents from the assault. Her laugh exposed his inability to persuade, to shift the blame away from his crimes.

"A good kid?" Vicky asked with a wave of her frail hand. Dirt dislodged from her fingertips and landed into Tony's eye. Even with overwhelming fear, and overwhelming pain controlling his body, the tiny bit assaulting his eye hurt like a bitch. "If I was *so* bad to you, then how do you explain how, now, you torture and bully all those other kids? The things you do to other now, is leaps and bounds worse than I ever did. You are sadistic. You are evil. You're a parasite disguised as a saint; feeding on the weak."

Tony screamed for help: perhaps this attempt to exit a nightmare would work. He didn't deserve to die. He was the victim; he was helping people; or helping society get rid of the weak.

"So, Tony, now, the small and weak will feed on you."

"Please, no. Please!" Tony pleaded through tears. His skin tore more-and-more as his body shook uncontrollably, the dolls didn't budge; so, his body paid the price.

Vicky grabbed her temples, as Tony watched – confused. She ripped her scalp apart on either side, the seam exposing a second beastly head beneath that of a frail haunting girl. Vicky's body now housed a black-ooze covered head with beady red-eyes, a long snout, and a mouth full of large, sharp teeth.

Tony clenched his eyes shut, hoping that the visual absence would removed him from this nightmare. But, his sense of smell kept him grounded in the hellish scene: The beast smelled of fermented shit mixed with a nauseating undertone of chicken-farm after a long weekend without clearing the carcasses. So, Tony came out of the darkness, and took in the sight before him, equally disgusting as the smell.

The beast smiled a hellish nonverbal, *hello,* and dropped down over Tony's body, holding posture inches above his face.

Ooze fell onto Tony's cheeks, sizzling the skin, and rolling to the ground. Tony pleaded to God and his mother for rescue.

He felt the warmth of urine pool in his pants, fear took full command of his faculties.

"Please don't let this happen. Please." Tony pleaded to the heavens in hopes for a response since Hell obviously had hold of his life and soul.

"Just be glad I got to you before the clown. You bullied the wrong kid," The beast laughed. "…had Scott's keeper got to you before me; this would have ended a lot worse." The beast finished.

"What does that little fuck have to do with anything?" Tony screamed, yearning to sound tough through tears and confusion. Scott was a weird little fucker; Tony tried to get him on track, but never thought Scott would pull anything like this. Scott was nothing more than a crazy loser that believed in imaginary friends – who the fuck wants a clown as a friend anyways? Walking around school with his idiot friends talking about their stupid D&D group: The Devil's Assassins. Tony must've been dreaming, things were well past the limits of reality.

Vicky's hands grabbed the skin of her head, returning the skin hood atop her body, covering the beast, and returning her back to the helm.

How many nightmares can one-person travel through? Tony's sense of reality was past fracture; permanently broken, unable to differentiate the events and consequences before.

"Sorry for the delay. He wanted to tell you that," Vicky chuckled. The sweet, innocent laugh that annoyed Tony years ago, now morphed into a horrifying shrill. "Now, how about we get started?"

Vicky gave a nod of approval toward her pets, her demeanor almost giddy at what was to come. A look that encompassed the thoughts of every person ever hurt by Tony, a unified stance of pleasure, of bloodlust.

The dolls reacted like piranha, devouring the entirety of Tony's body. The crunching of bone could be heard from within and out; pain overloaded the scene. Mother Nature surely retreated, nauseated.

Tony's screams turned into gargled shrieks as blood filled his throat and pooled in his mouth. Vicky's laugh drowned his screams; all Tony could hear was the shrill laughter and sounds of dolls devouring his body. He attempted to flail, but, one-by-one, limbs he couldn't move became limbs he couldn't feel. Was his pain physical or situational; he couldn't be sure anymore; death had to follow shortly; right? Within minutes he was nothing more than a head, lying on the meadow's floor.

The dolls pulled from the ground and returned to the door. Blood ran down their cloth, plastic, and porcelain faces leaving a crimson path from Tony to the door. One-by-one they disappeared below, their laughs echoing below.

Vicky retrieved Tony – or rather his head – from the ground and held it out front of her: eye-level. Tony's lifeless head – or wishfully lifeless – gave a large gasp for air and his eyes darted for reality, finally focusing on Vicky, full of fear – no reality in sight.

"What is going on? Why can't I move?" Tony asked.

Vicky tossed Tony in the sky.

Tony exploded into a shock-induced chuckle, he was nothing more than a head! His laughter, or rather volume, ascended and descended with each throw: tumbling over-and-over in the sky, touching heaven and being pulled back to hell.

Vicky returned him to her arms and held him up again. "You didn't think you got to die that easy, did you? You're coming with me; you're my plaything, to tease, from now on."

Laughter quickly escaped, making room for screams for help, muffled by the sounds of Vicky's laughter. He had come to terms with the night's events, but to repeat the events, instead of meeting a silent death was unacceptable, torturous even. So, he continued his wails; wails for help, for release, for death; wails for anything other than what waited below, with Vicky. They approached the opening and his fear peaked. If he had a heart, he surely would have suffered a heart attack. But instead he just screamed, wishing he never walked into the forest.

Vicky gave Tony one more kiss on the forehead and dropped him into the abyss. The sounds of his screaming faded as he plummeted. He watched as Vicky climbed down, grabbing the door and closing it behind her.

With the door shut tight, the sounds and horrors ceased. Silence signaled a return to reality; Widow Forest absorbed the Cellar Door once again. With the Cellar Door contained beneath the core, silence gave way to the sounds of the forest, as if nothing happened.

Chelsea

"Come on, you don't have to be scared," Chelsea poked. "You're with me, nothing's going to happen with an adult around?" Her new friend Chad wasn't as willing to enter the infamous Widow Forest as she hoped. Chelsea parked her car at the edge of Widow Forest to escape civilization, in desperate need for privacy. The sounds of sirens chanted in the distance, calming Chelsea, since it meant authorities were elsewhere. She moved away from her run-down Chevy Caviler—just another indication of her low-class demeanor—toward the tree line. She gave Chad a smile and *come-hither* wave.

Chad released his hold of the car and followed. "Chelsea, I do trust you, but everyone knows to stay away from Widow Forest. You're new here. Just trust me, please," Chad pleaded as he advanced. But Chelsea continued, only looking over her shoulder to ensure his obedience.

Chelsea had overheard the night before that Chad had grazed the occasional boob, even grabbed an ass. Meaning, she would be able to manipulate his hormonal urges for her own. Chelsea was willing to go *all the way*, something she made sure her teenage suitor was aware of by donning a top that exposed the bounce of her tits with each exaggerated step, and, by *accidentally* grazing his *never-touched* regions.

The two had met the day before at a local high school party. A few kids stopped her out front of a gas station and asked her to buy them alcohol, minutes after she helped Stacey with her *lack-of-alcohol* problem.

Chelsea's irresponsible behavior outweighed any normal logic held by a 24-year-old. No, she was the worst type of predator: irresponsible, stupid, and entitled. Irresponsible with the innocences of young men she manipulated. Stupid enough to believe she wasn't in the wrong. And, entitled with the belief that she was the victim—no matter what. So, she bounced from town to town, contributing drugs and alcohol to underage boys for an invitation to secluded hangouts, free from—proper—adult supervision. And after she snatched from them innocence and mental stability, she demanded money and pity. She lacked the mental capacity, honesty, and drive to make it in a world full of adults, so she immersed herself with like-minded individuals: children.

Chad caught her eye that night. Standing alone on the sidelines while everyone else worshipped her childish behavior and inhibitions. Young men dream of an older woman like Chelsea, one that is willing to show them things only wet dreams expose. But Chad was her favorite type of *man*, one that let her command the show. While other boys rallied around to stare at her momentarily exposed bosom or to receive a smooch, Chad stayed in the back, shy and quiet. So, when the party ended she made sure Chad had a ride home and they made plans to meet the next night.

"Oh stop, don't tell me you believe in hocus-pocus stuff. You're smarter than those other dumb-dumbs." Chelsea replied.

She grabbed Chad's arm and pulled him in tight, making sure he felt the heat of her chest against his body. His demeanor shifted, calmed even—she won. She had to leave in a few days but refused to spend the time alone, so she needed his *company* until then. Besides, his preppy clothing and building wallet had to mean he came from money, and gas money wasn't easy to come by for the immature and lazy. So, she claimed her control and turned around, rubbing her round ass against his teenage cock.

"Okay, now that you're calm, let's go somewhere private," She coerced.

"Why? You look young enough to be a kid, if someone sees us they won't be able to tell how old you are." Chad replied. Chelsea was easily a foot shorter than Chad, standing 5-foot 1-inch, and never lost her baby face, so he was right.

"True, but if anyone catches us doing the things I want to do they are gonna ask for ID's to tell our parents how *naughty* we are." Chelsea said gliding her hands down Chad's chest and giving his crotch a gentle squeeze. He let out a small moan sending her into a tailspin. She jumped into his arms and bit his neck; she ran her tongue across the goosebumps that rose from his skin.

"Okay, but we can't go to far. The forest is really dense, and it is dark, we don't want to get lost in there," Chad whispered through moans. "Besides, I promise you, no one is coming out here."

"Deal!" Chelsea exclaimed. "I don't plan on getting you lost in the forest, just lost in *me*." She could feel his package throb at the idea of being inside her.

"Let's go!" She commanded.

Full-sprint, Chelsea ran into the woods, hoping for a game of cat-and-mouse foreplay. But, like most of her plans in life, it failed. Chad caught up moments later—lazy mentality equals lazy physique. She forced an exaggerated pout, seeking unneeded comfort. She quickly retracted the lip whimper when Chad looked confused, trading the action for Chad's hand in fright—damsel in distress.

The two travelled inward, hand-in-hand, with rays of moonlight illuminating the obstacles in their path. A few times Chad tried to let go of Chelsea's hand when the terrain required single-file travel, but Chelsea wouldn't let go. She had leeched on and wouldn't be expelled till she found her next enabler.

Chad broke the silence and asked, "So where are you from?"

Chelsea tensed. She didn't like talking about reality. Sure, she had left a kid, and maybe she isn't a functioning member of society, but none of that was her fault. So, instead she played with children, where she could be in charge and feel like the smartest—something she never could achieve in *reality*.

"Nowhere really. My family threw me away when I was four and my adopted parents hit me, called me names, and made sure I know I am worthless." Chelsea explained in a *woe-is-me* baby voice.

"You mean knew?" Chad added.

"What?" Chelsea asked, confused.

"You said they hit you, called you names, and made sure you *know* you are worthless; don't you mean made sure you *knew* you *were* worthless." Chad replied.

"Whatever, I didn't realize my pain required an English lesson," Chelsea whined.

"Grammar lesson, and I'm not saying that, it just stuck out, it was weird." Chad retorted snatching his hand back to rub his eyes.

"You know, maybe you should stick to your nice life, with your nice family, and leave my fucked up past out of it!" Chelsea defended, her anger would have been properly received had she not flailed about in the thralls of a temper-tantrum, the only proof of her adulthood being the constant jiggling and near exposure of her tits. "Not all of us got to go to a smart school and have a nice family."

"Yeah, sure. Just be quiet for a minute."

They stopped, lost in the middle of the forest, staring at each other, and let silence weigh-in on the situation. Chelsea had seen the expression on Chad's face before, the face men made when they didn't believe her or thought she was stupid. Everyone thought she was dumb, but she wasn't, she was smart—or so she believed. The only trait Chelsea had equal to her stupidity was her damaged soul. And the world was to blame. She deserved everything she wanted, she deserved complete devotion from *men*—like Chad.

"Look, I'm going home. I don't think this is a good idea. I'm not even supposed to be out here. Let's go back." Chad commanded.

Just like all the people in Chelsea's past, he thought he was better than her and could tell her what to do. Chelsea produced tears, something she learned to do on command; she needed him to worship her. And as a true predator she unwilling to let her prey get away.

Chelsea tried to salvage the situation and regain control; "Let's just have our fun here, I'm sorry, it was stupid, and I want to make it better."

She moved in close, again, and grabbed his hand. Slowly she raised it then shoved it down her top till she felt his ring finger graze her nipple. She fondled the crotch of his jeans with her other hand. But he wasn't excited anymore.

Chad pulled away shaking his head; "You're crazy. Look let's just pretend this never happened." He pulled his phone out and made a call as he walked away.

"Mom, can you meet me at Grant's house in thirty minutes...Thanks."

Chelsea watched Chad walk away, watched as another judgmental *man* walked away, it wasn't fair.

She yelled out; "Fuck you Chad! Your lucky I don't get the cops to come after you for using me!"

Chad called back, over his shoulder, "Want me to call my mom back so you can tell her...didn't think so." Then he was gone from Chelsea's sight. Moments later silence broke as he yelled out, "You need help!"

Chelsea collapsed under the weight of her own despair. Yet again she was alone. So, what if she made some stuff up? No one ever cared unless her life was a sad story. All she wanted was for someone to take care of her, to prove devotion by believing her stories and accepting her behavior. Her mother and father never believed her, either. No one could prove she was lying so they should all love and believe her. Even Justin, the father of her baby, wouldn't accept her and always wanted too much. Fuck adulting.

Chelsea collapsed to the ground and whispered to the sky.

"No one cares about me, no one ever takes my side." The words disappeared into the night air faster than the chance of them being true. Deep down she knew she was a bad person, a lazy person, a conniving person. But none of that mattered. Only she knew those facts, everyone else was simply judging her without cause.

She jumped, startled when a voice asked *anyone there.* Searching for the voice's owner she eyed a boyish figure walking aimlessly, in the distance, the only trait she could make out was his muscles trapped under a tight shirt. And like *that* she forgot about Chad, and her woes. The idea of attaching to another person exciting her parasite of a soul. She ran—what she called running—after him, calling out, but he disappeared into the night. He should have heard her, why didn't he stop? He was probably a friend of Chad's and now they were playing games with her.

"So, what...you guys gonna rape me?" Chelsea called out. No reply.

The forest around her all looked the same, so much so that she couldn't remember the direction of her car, or the exit. She spun around, around again disorienting herself trying to find a clue or trace of her previous steps. The moonlight faded as fast as her ability to stand, consumed by fear and grasping at relief in the fetal position.

"Chad's phone had service!" Chelsea squeaked. She retrieved her pre-paid cellphone tucked in-between her breasts. All-too-quickly she realized her cheap phone didn't produce the same level of serviceability. Since she had no idea which way led back to her car, she decided to follow the cellphone tower Gods, waving her phone about as she traveled aimlessly for a *bar*.

"Come on, stupid phone. All I need is one bar."

The moon dipped down away from Chelsea, almost as if it wanted no part of the trouble she was heading toward. Chelsea stayed her pursuit for service, ignoring the environmental sense of warning. She was alone with the few wits she had about her. Her body played victim to the oblivious pursuit. Before long she bore small cuts and bruises from collisions with trees and brush. Apparently, Mother Nature was *actually* Father Flora since only men assaulted her with such disregard. She stumbled over roots and brush as the forest thickened around her. Her peripheral vision collapsed as she stared at the bright unnatural light of her phone and darkness strengthened around her.

The last strand of hope flickered, died in deadly unison when her phone died, taking with it clear sight and the notion of safety. A childish pout and tantrum coupled the realization. The sounds of nature drowned with screams and pleads. Over-and-over without even waiting for response, she screamed for help. Before long, her voice denied use, her tear ducts tapped out, and her body shut down. She couldn't fight any longer, she submitted and slid to the ground. Her tears and whimpers slowly faded to heavy breaths—sleep.

****

How long had she slept? Couldn't have been long since the moon was still high in the night sky. However, the visibility level had improved. She rose with a stretch and wiped the crusted sleep and tears from her eyes, smearing her already atrocious make-up job into a bad case of *raccoon eyes.*

The wind nipped at her belly button and inner thighs, but why? She ran her hands down her body—her shirt and pants were gone. Fear chased sleep out of her mind and took the helm. She looked down at her exposed pink bra that was two sizes too small and her jet-black panties: where had her pants and shirt gone? Never mind the fact that she wasn't in the middle of the forest anymore. She was in a clearing where the moon had decided to take a front row seat for the show.

Fear was the next emotion pushed from the throne of Chelsea's mind, conceding to confusion. There was nothing to fear: no people, animals, or injury. So, confusion settled in. Obviously, this was nothing more than an elaborate prank, one she would surely share with her next host as emotionally damaging material.

"Can I have my clothes back now?" Chelsea screamed, hands on her hips, attempting to command control—no response. If asking wasn't going to work she would try another trick. She turned to the nearest edge of trees and slapped a large smile on her face.

"Come on boys. We can still have fun!" She pulled her tits out and fondled her nipples; in her head it was the most glorious sight any young boy could hope to see. However, if she took an honest look into a second-rate motel mirror, she would realize she was actually a rundown, unattractive, uneducated, pathetic, whitetrash parasite.

Chelsea was too busy rubbing her chest and yelling at imaginary boys to hear or sense the movement occurring behind her. Therefore, the shock to her heart was concentrated and fast, thundering instead of slow-building when she turned to find a small girl and four large gluttonous men.

The four men were exact copies of each other. They stood well over 6-feet tall, and most likely were the same length around. They wore skintight white tank-top undershirts that hugged every excessive bodily roll. The shirts were covered in brown stains and dripping with sweat. None of them wore clothing on their bottom halves leaving their bulbous erections, wet at the tip, exposed and throbbing in Chelsea's direction. Their bodies were those of 40 or 50-year-old men, but just north of the multiple chins each man possessed a haunting baby-face.

Chelsea thought the faces were masked, but when they started winking, licking their lips, and moaning the gruesome truth set-in. Two men were on either side of the little girl, all of them hand-in-hand. The little girl, with long, brown hair matching her big, brown eyes, seemed oddly familiar. She smiled at Chelsea as if the monstrous men weren't even there. At that moment Chelsea made her first smart decision in years: she put her tits away—too little, too late.

Chelsea tripped over words and actions as her mind overloaded from the scene.

Finally, she spat out; "Little girl, come here so we can get out of here."

The men didn't seem to be doing much of anything except standing there, so maybe she could grab the girl and make a run for it—at least, what she called running. She looked around quickly for her clothes, one last time, but gave up; she had to keep eyes on the monsters in front of her, her mind and body reminded her of that, each nerve firing a warning due to the creepy stares of the creatures.

"Why do we need to leave, Mommy?" The little girl asked.

Chelsea zoned in on the little girl's face, the gears in her head spun. The smile, eyes, and nose were all there, but it couldn't've been her; Jessica was surely at home, with her dad, in bed.

"You're not Jessica." Chelsea took a step back from the five of them, frantically shaking her head. With each step she took, they followed as if in-tow.

"Of course I am, Mommy. You just don't know me cause you left, cause you're a bitch of a mommy." Jessica replied mater-of-factly with a chuckle. "Besides, it doesn't matter…don't you like my friends?"

"I don't understand. What is happening right now, Jessica?" Chelsea wanted nothing more than to return to reality. Something she had not wished in a very long time, but now she wanted nothing more than to beat down the door of reality till someone opened it and dead-bolted it shut behind her.

"Well, it is time for you to get what you want and what you deserve, at the same time. You get to have your cake and eat it too, Mommy." Jessica explained. "Since you never wanted me or daddy, except as an excuse for pity, or blame, I just wanted to show you I am a bigger person. At four-years-old I am more mature than you, Mommy, and I am going to give you a present."

Jessica clapped her hands and the pack of men stepped forward. The ground shook with each step, crippling Chelsea to the ground. The men opened their mouths and the voices of Chelsea's victims emitted. Like recordings playing over each other, the air was filled with familiar inappropriate conversations and teenage moans. Moans that Chelsea demanded from her suitors, now she denounced and detested from the grotesque monsters. Through the roars and earthly shakes Chelsea could still make-out Jessica's voice, clear as day:

"You like to rape little boys, Mommy? You like to tell lies about your past? Well now you will have one truly bad story to tell the devil, but not anyone else. Have fun Mommy."

Jessica pulled two stuffed dolls from behind her back—one looked like a clown, the other a boy. She sat on the ground and played; absent minded—as a child should—and without regard of the horrific scene before her.

The grotesque men circled Chelsea. Each putting a foot on her body, pinning her to the ground.

She tried to move but couldn't. The only thing she could do was panic, she finally understood what true fear and assault felt like. She screamed and clamored for release, but not as a controlled response, no, this was real terror taking over. The toes of each foot pinning her to the ground stretched across her body, like snakes they slithered atop her skin. Two ripped her panties and bra off, then they all started groping and inserting into her body—she screamed in dismay. The men smiled, surely from the feel of her flesh and the sounds of her screams, they stroked their ever-inflating members.

The moans of her victims played over-and-over, louder-and-louder, as the monsters stroked harder and faster. Toes—snake(ish) toes, that is—dug deeper into her skin as the monstrous men tensed up and shivered. Chelsea tensed, as well, because she knew what was coming, they were *cumming*, and she didn't want it, not this time, not like this. Her body was on fire with *real* responses to the horrific scene. Her heart tried to leave her chest, over and over, so much so that it caused her pain. Something should couldn't fake in the past; something she didn't realize was possible. How could her body be working against her at a time such as this?

All four heads—penis heads—pulsed trying to move the cum up the shaft and onto her body. In unison, the moans turned to grunts. The men came, but instead of the warm milky liquid Chelsea expected, the men ejaculated oozy black pools onto her skin. For a moment her tears calmed feeling the worst was done. But what was moving across her body?

Chelsea peered down her body at the black, oozy baby-juice in horror. Each stream slithered across her being. The puddles separated, thinned, and continued across her skin toward a destination and burrowed into her skin, feeding off the evilness inside. Chelsea screamed in agony with each progressive chomp.

"Please, stop!" Chelsea pleaded. The men walked away and disappeared down a hole on the other side of the clearing. Jessica, however, advanced to Chelsea's body.

The demonic leeches grew larger with every second. The concentrated evil and selfishness of Chelsea was *mother's milk* for them. Her body exasperated in anguish, she had lost control, entirely. Her body, her soul, her will, was no longer hers to command.

"Mommy, you were a parasite on this world, one of the worst kind."

"Don't you mean *are?*" Chelsea pleaded again, holding on to hope.

Jessica grabbed Chelsea by the foot and drug her toward the opening in the ground across the clearing.

"No, I meant *were,* Mommy. You're already dead. And from now on you will be food for all kinds of parasites and demons, doesn't that sound fun?"

Chelsea tried to pull away, but Jessica was unnaturally strong. She tried pulling the leeches from her skin, but they only dug deeper, worsening the pain. She tried clawing at the ground, but only lost poorly-polished nails in the process. With each nail that strained and ripped from bed, she screamed in pain, and watched in horror as they made trail of her captors route. A physical piece that would remain while her screams and being faded to nothing.

Jessica sat Chelsea up to look inside the hole. Heat blasted her face, she got the hint—she knew what waited below. Jessica let out one last laugh that chilled Chelsea's soul in the presence of Hell's fire.

Jessica's laugh quickly turned deep, gargled, and demonic. Chelsea turned around and Jessica's eyes transformed red and her skin was melting by way of black ooze. With one last action Jessica kicked Chelsea into the abyss, and Chelsea silently fell below, all air evacuated from her lungs.

"I'll be your sugar daddy, Bitch!" Yelled the demon, finished stripping away the façade of Jessica's skin.

The demon crawled back into the hole and pulled the door shut. The Cellar Door disappeared again into the night. The moon quickly hid behind clouds like a child under the blankets hoping to evade horror. One beam poked out from behind clouded shroud, almost as if on purpose, shedding light on a sign just on the edge of the forest, warning all that pass to…

Stay out! The Cellar Door awaits its next victim!

-The End-

93563930R00057

Made in the USA
Columbia, SC
11 April 2018